WHERE'S THE BABY?

a spotting book

Britta Teckentrup

These chattering parrots
so high in the tree,
are a rainbow of colour –
lovely to see.

They hop and they flutter;
you'll have to be quick,
to see the bright parrot
who's hiding her chick.

Under the ocean,
so still and so blue,
the orca are singing –
can you hear them too?

There's a mother and calf
who swim side by side,
but the little one's shy
and he's trying to hide.

All round the farmyard
hens flutter and cluck.
Does one have a baby?
You might be in luck!

For hiding inside
one hen's cosy nest,
is a fluffy young chick
snuggled close to her chest.

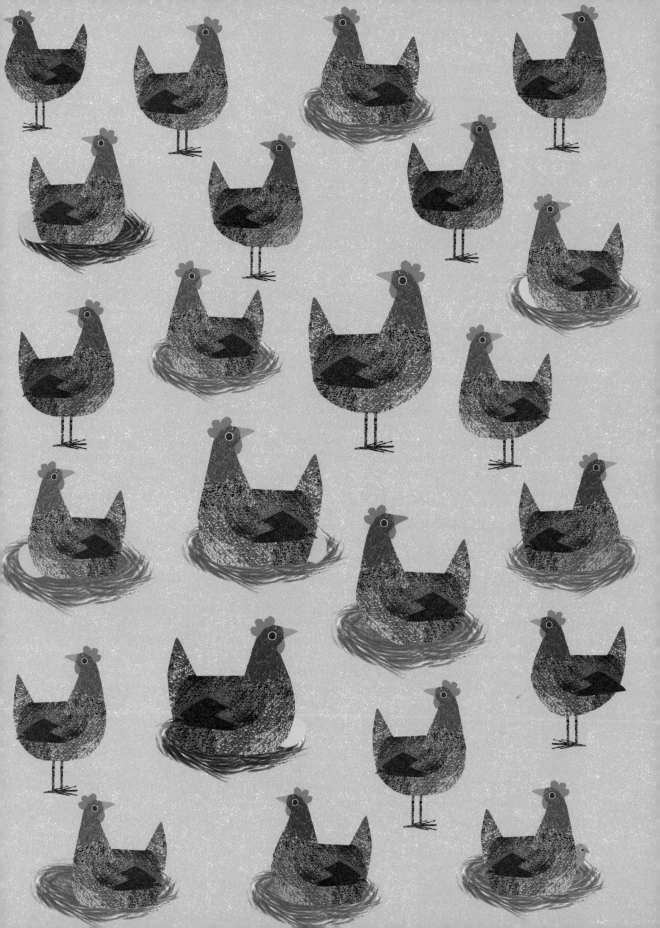

These slumbering sloths
love hanging around
in the tops of the trees,
so high off the ground.

Where's the sloth baby?
Does anyone know?
You've got time to look
because sloths are so slow!

These geese swim about
in the blue of the lake,
honking and splashing –
the noise that they make!

And paddling beside
her mum in the water
is a young gosling –
the goose's new daughter!

Hunting and creeping
through tall jungle trees,
these tigers' bold stripes
make them tricky to see.

But look once again
at these tigers, so wild,
and you'll see the one
with a small tiger child.

With trumpeting trunks
and thundering feet,
elephants march through
the still desert heat.

And right by his mum
with his skin just as grey,
is an elephant calf
who is running to play.

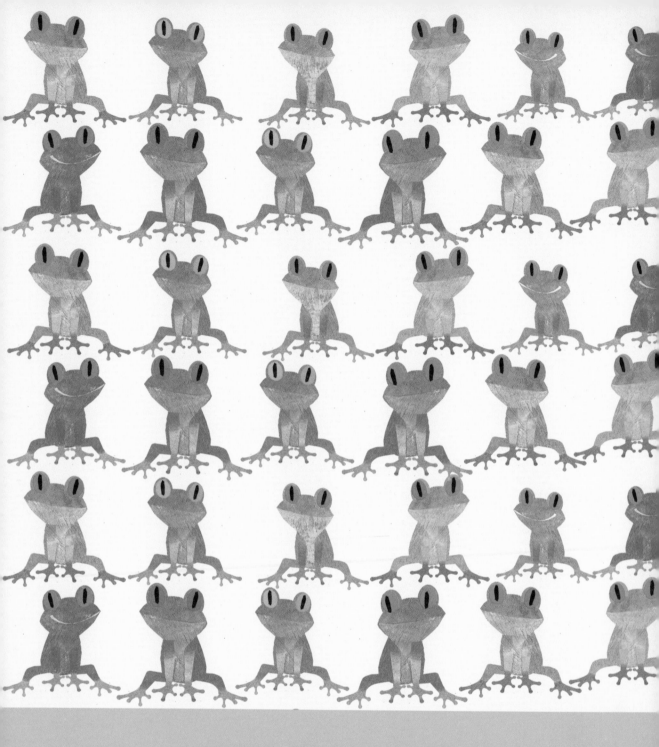

These frogs like to climb
in the tallest tree tops.
Through the rainforest leaves
they leap and they hop.

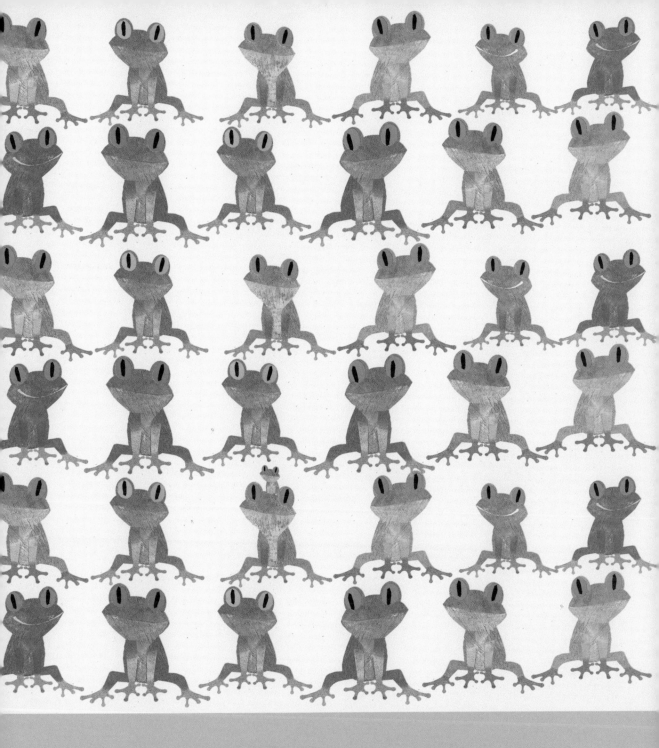

There's a small tree frog baby
with friendly red eyes,
whose mum's bright green back
is the perfect disguise!

They're the colour of dust,
like the dry outback sand.
They're not easy to find
in this hot, arid land.

These kangaroos move
with great jumps and leaps,
and one has a pouch
where a small joey peeps.

This herd of giraffes
on the African plains,
have long, spotty necks
and short, stripy manes.

Are you able to spot
the mother giraffe?
If you look closely
you'll see her new calf.

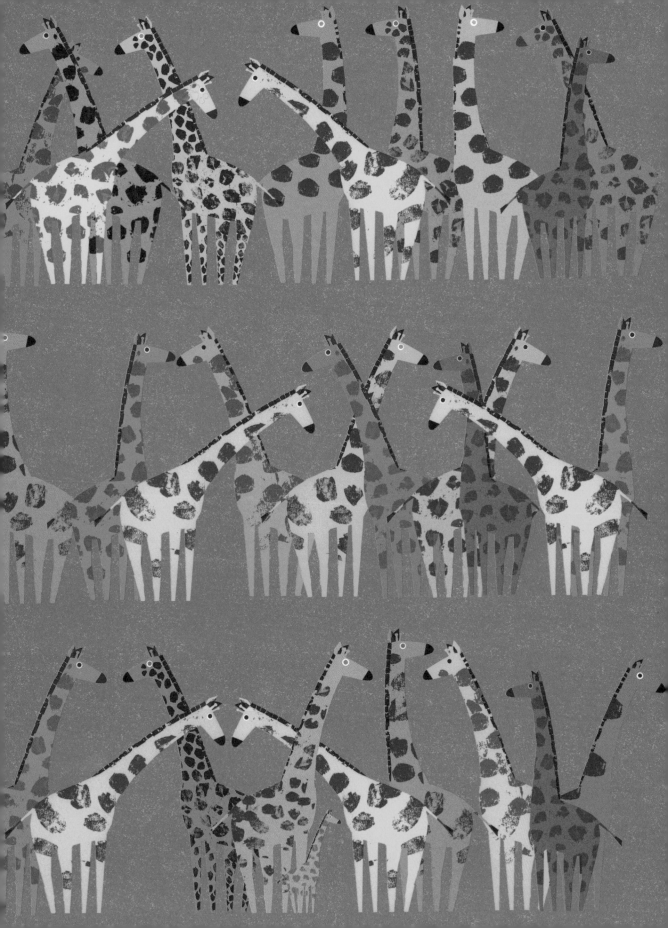

Look in a rock pool
when it is low tide
and you will see seahorses
swimming inside.

Where is the baby?
He's deep in the pool,
where the still, salty water
is peaceful and cool.

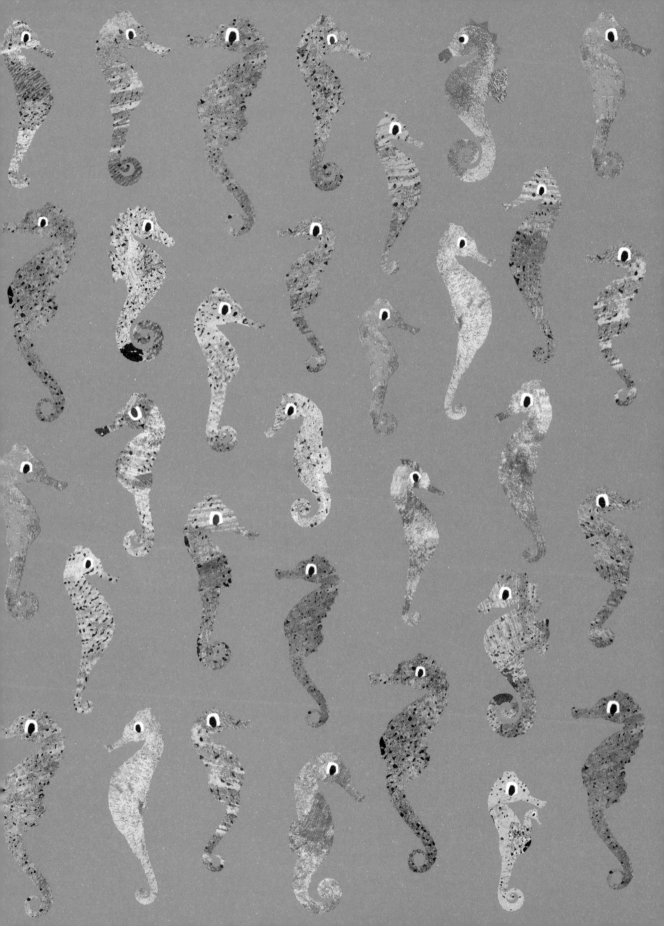

**Black and white zebras
gallop and run –
across the savannah
beneath the hot sun.**

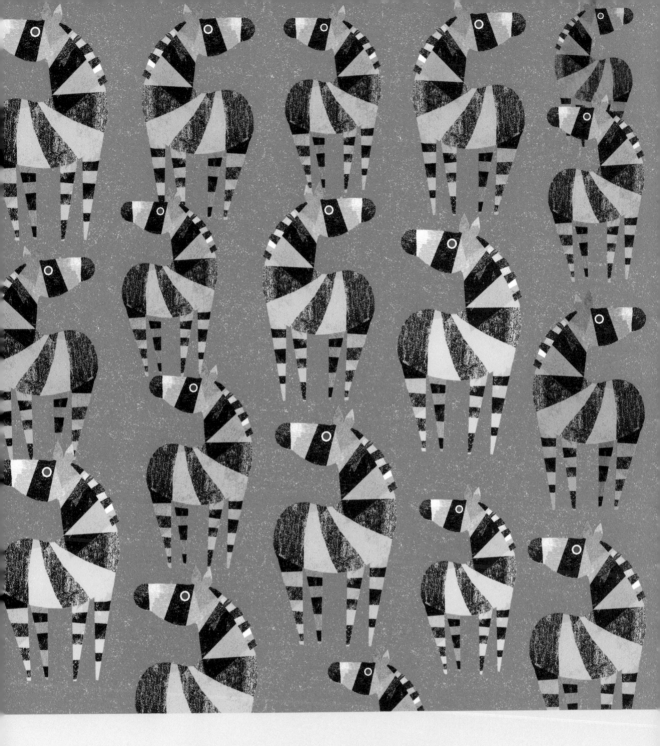

There's a new zebra foal,
who is hiding from you.
She runs with the herd
and she's black and white too!

Their teeth are so sharp
and they snap and they chomp.
You'll have to be careful
if you're near the swamp!

There's a mother here too
with a small crocodile,
which she carefully holds
with a big, toothy smile.

Snails slither and slide
all over the place.
They're not very fast and
they won't win a race.

And riding in style
on the shell of his mum
is a little snail baby –
can you see the one?

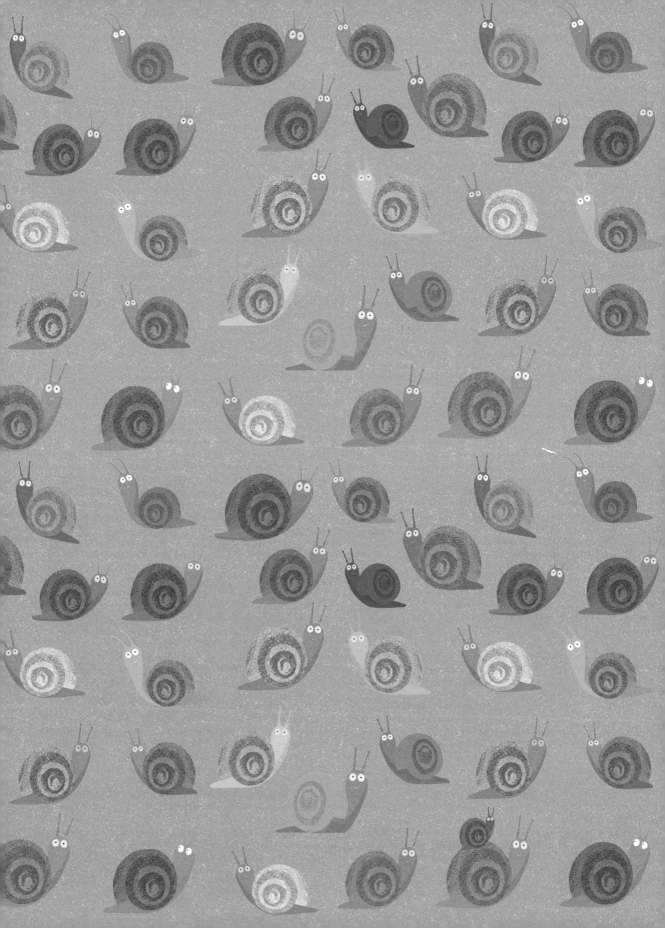

Here are the babies
and here are the mothers,
but is there a young one
with sisters or brothers?

Among stripes and spots
and colourful fins,
can you see the mother
whose babies are TWINS?

BIG PICTURE PRESS

First published in the UK in 2017 by Big Picture Press,
part of the Bonnier Publishing Group,
The Plaza, 535 King's Road, London, SW10 0SZ
www.bonnierpublishing.com

1 3 5 7 9 10 8 6 4 2

ISBN 978-1-78370-610-5

This book was typeset in Brown.
The illustrations were created digitally.

Written and edited by Katie Haworth
Designed by Winsome d'Abreu
Printed in China